MOONGAME

FRANK ASCH

PICTURE CORGI BOOKS

**Also by Frank Asch and published by
Picture Corgi Books:—**

**HAPPY BIRTHDAY MOON
MOONCAKE
JUST LIKE DADDY
THE LAST PUPPY
SANDCAKE**

To Devin, Amanda, Rachel, Megan, Sam, Caleb,
Jeremy, Lindsey, Chris, Daniel, and Luke

MOONGAME
A PICTURE CORGI BOOK   0 552 524433

Originally published in U.S.A. by Prentice-Hall, Inc.
First published in Great Britain by Hodder and Stoughton
Children's Books

PRINTING HISTORY
Hodder and Stoughton edition published 1985
Picture Corgi edition published 1987

Copyright © Frank Asch 1984

Picture Corgi Books are published by Transworld Publishers Ltd.,
61-63 Uxbridge Road, Ealing, London W5 5SA, in Australia by
Transworld Publishers (Australia) Pty. Ltd., 15-23 Helles Avenue,
Moorebank, NSW 2170, and in New Zealand by Transworld
Publishers (N.Z.) Ltd. Cnr. Moselle and Waipareira Avenues,
Henderson, Auckland.

Made and printed in Portugal by Printer Portugesa

One day, Little Bird showed Bear a new game: hide and seek. First he told Bear to hide and counted to ten: 1, 2, 3, 4, 5, 6, 7, 8, 9, 10. Then he went looking for Bear.

"I found you!" chirped Little Bird when
  he found Bear hiding behind some bushes.
"Now it's your turn to find me!"
  All day long, until the sun went down,
  Bear and Little Bird played their new game.

That night when Bear was all alone he
looked up in the sky and said to the moon,
"Let's play hide and seek!
First I'll hide and you find me."

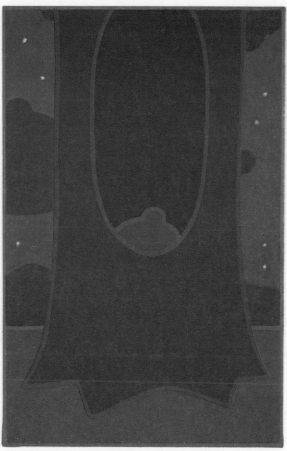

Then Bear ran as fast as he could
until he came to an old hollow tree.
Climbing inside, he ducked down
so the moon couldn't see him.

Bear waited for a while, then he poked his
head up. When he did, the moon was right
there looking down at him.
"Okay," said Bear, "you found me.
Now it's your turn to hide."
Closing his eyes, Bear began to count
just as Little Bird had shown him.

At that moment a gentle breeze

slowly hid the moon behind a big cloud.

When Bear finished counting, he set out
to find the moon. First he thought he
found the moon hiding behind some rocks.

Then he thought he found the moon
hiding in someone's house.

When Bear thought he found the moon hiding
in a tree he shook the tree and cried,
"I found you, Moon!"
But Bear was mistaken.
All he found was a big balloon.

Then Little Bird came by to visit.

"Will you help me find the moon?" asked Bear.

"Sure, I'll help," chirped Little Bird.

Bear and Little Bird looked and looked

but they couldn't find the moon.

So they went to the forest to ask for help.
"I think the moon is lost," explained Bear.
"Can you help me find him?"
"Don't worry, we'll help you,"
replied the animals in the forest.

Together they searched and searched.

But they couldn't find the moon.

At last, Bear sat down and sighed,

"The moon is lost, and it's all my fault!"

Then Bear got an idea.

He jumped up and cried,

"Okay, Moon, I give up. You win!"

Just then the breeze began to blow again,

and the moon came out of its hiding place.

"Look," chirped Little Bird, "The moon wasn't lost.
He was just hiding behind that big cloud."
Bear was so happy he danced and danced.

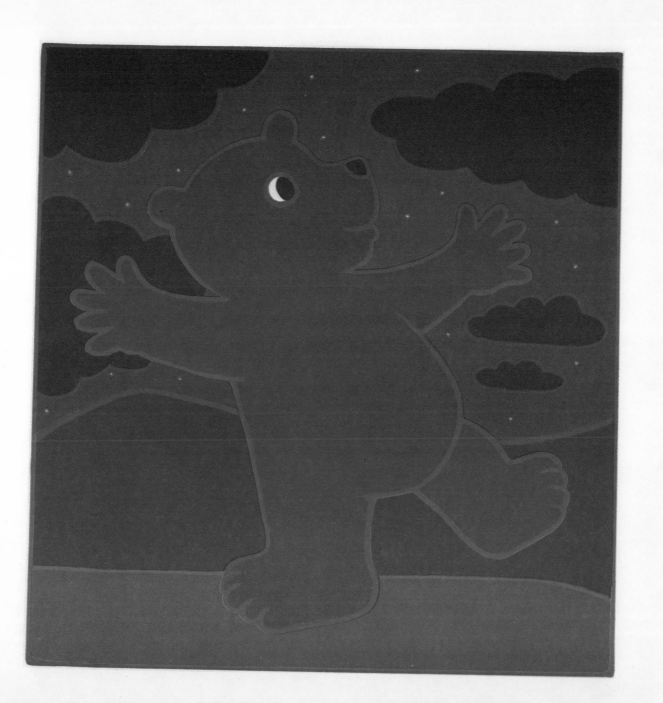

Then everyone played hide and seek.